W9-DJC-705

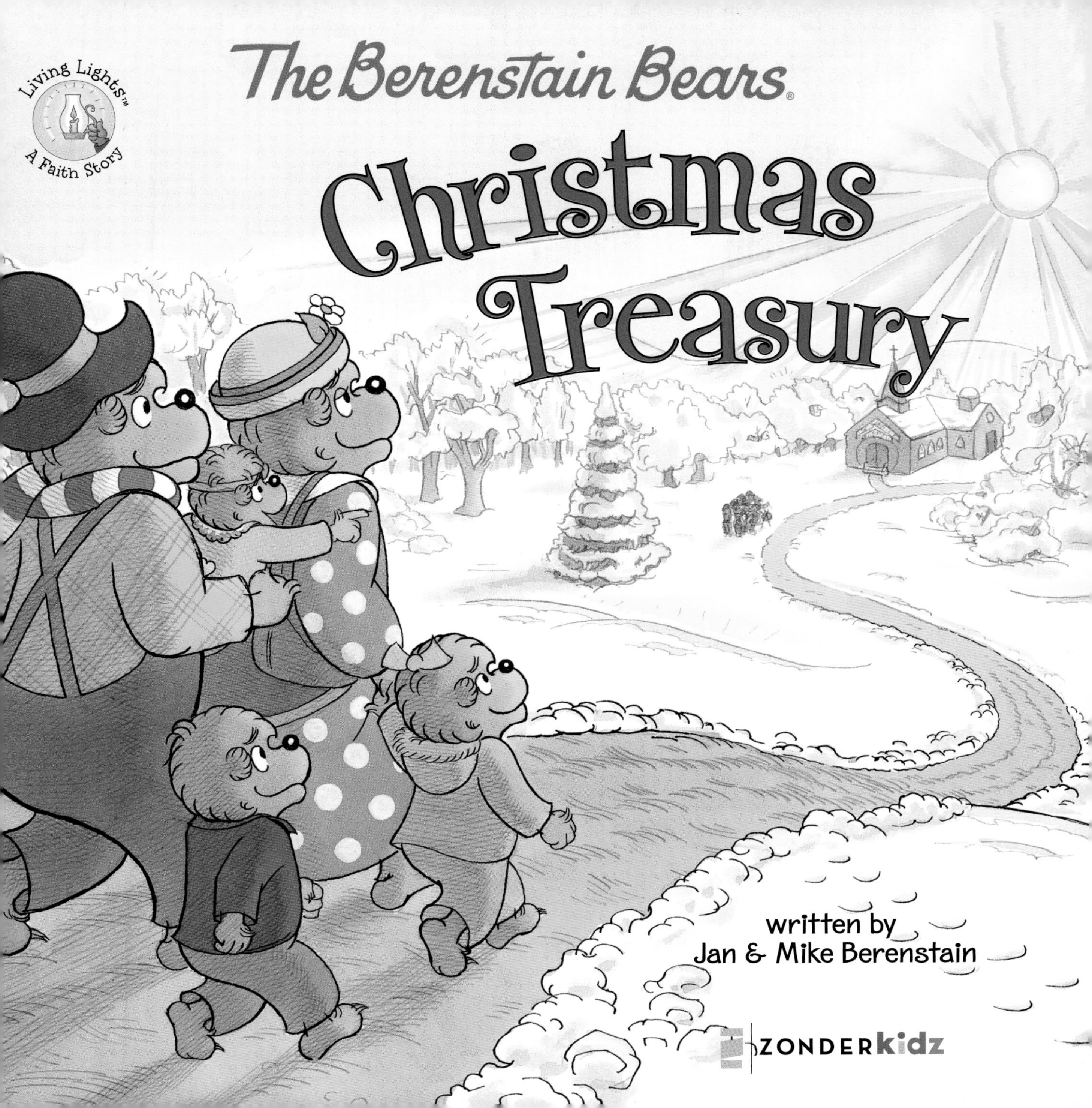
Living Lights™
A Faith Story
The Berenstain Bears®
Christmas Treasury
written by
Jan & Mike Berenstain
ZONDERkidz

ZONDERKIDZ

The Berenstain Bears® and the Christmas Angel
ISBN 978-0-310-74924-0

The Berenstain Bears® and the Joy of Giving I
SBN 978-0-310-71255-8

The Berenstain Bears® The Very First Christmas
ISBN 978-0-310-75102-1

Requests for information should be addressed to:

Zondervan, 3900 *Sparks Dr., Grand Rapids, Michigan 49546*

ISBN 978-0-310-62708-1 (hardcover)

Printed in China

16 17 18 19 20 21 DSC 6 5 4 3 2 1

written by
Jan & Mike Berenstain

TABLE OF CONTENTS

"The angel said to him, 'I am Gabriel. I stand in the presence of God, and I have been sent to speak to you and to tell you this good news.'"
—Luke 1:19

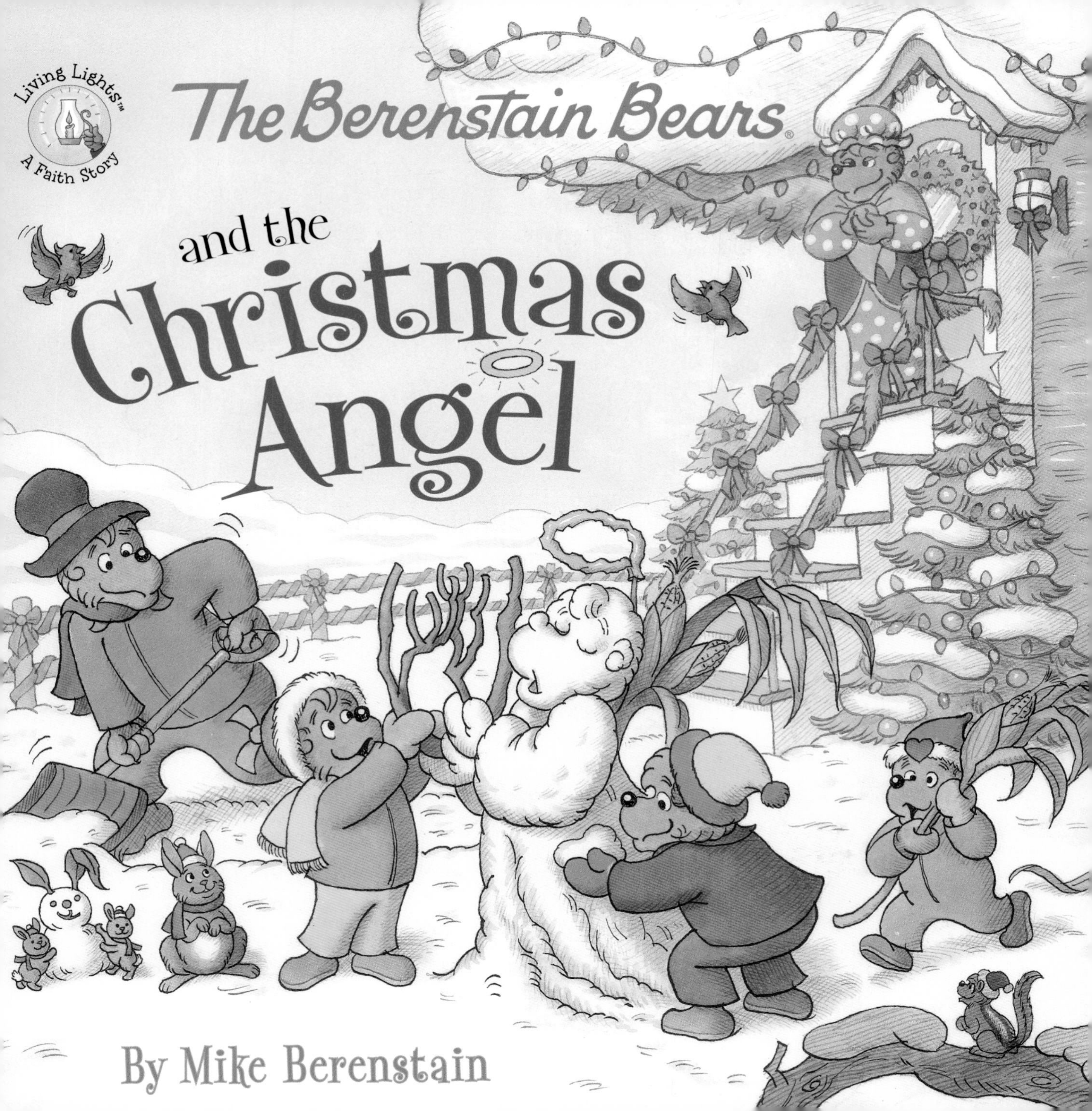
Living Lights™
A Faith Story
The Berenstain Bears®
and the
Christmas
Angel
By Mike Berenstain

It was the week before Christmas in Bear Country and winter was just settling in. There had already been some chilly weather. A few snow flurries had come and gone. One frosty morning, there had even been a light snowfall. Brother, Sister, and Honey had rushed outside to quickly try building a snowbear. But the snow melted as soon as the sun rose.

Now, the weather forecast finally said there would be several inches of snow overnight. The cubs were so excited they could hardly sleep. They lay awake imagining all the next day's snowy fun.

In the morning, sure enough, there was a snowy blanket on the ground and more snow was coming down.

"Hooray!" cried the cubs. "It's snowing! *It's snowing!* IT'S SNOWING!"

“Let’s go out right away to build a snowbear!” said Sister.

“Yes!” Brother and Honey agreed.

“Just a minute,” said Mama. “No one’s going anywhere without some breakfast.”

The cubs gobbled up their breakfast while gazing out the window at all that beautiful snow.

"Bye, Mama! Thanks!" they said as they swallowed a last gulp of milk. Then the cubs bundled into their snow clothes and bounded out the door.

At first, the cubs just stood there taking in the snowy scene. Bear Country was truly lovely cloaked all in white.

They tilted their heads back to feel the snow falling on their faces. They opened their mouths to catch the flakes on their tongues. Then, laughing, they plunged into the deep snow.

"Let's build that snowbear!" said Sister.

"Right!" said Brother and Honey.

"What kind of snowbear should we build?" wondered Sister.

"How about one with a corncob pipe, a button nose, and two eyes made out of coal?" asked Brother.

“And an old silk hat with a broomstick in his hand?” added Sister. “That’s so old school. Let’s try something different.”

"How about a modern-looking one with both eyes on one side of his head?" asked Brother.

"That's *too* different!" said Sister.

"Hmm," they all said, thinking it over.

While Brother and Sister were thinking, Honey got a little bored. She flopped down on her back in the snow, waving her arms and legs, making "snow angels." That gave Brother an idea.

"I know—we'll build a snow *angel*," he said. "A Christmas snow angel!"

"Good idea!" said Sister, getting excited. "We can give it wings, a halo, and a harp."

So they set to work. They rolled three big snowballs together for the body and head. They molded arms and flowing robes. They found a bent branch shaped like a harp and then used dried cornstalks for wings. Finally, the cubs bent an old coat hanger and covered it with shiny foil for the halo.

As the cubs finished their snow angel, Mama called them in for hot chocolate. Sipping their drinks, they admired their work through the kitchen window.

"That's a very fine snow angel," said Papa, joining them. "I think it must be Gabriel, the Christmas angel."

"Gabriel?" said Sister. "I didn't know angels have names."

"This one does," said Mama. She pointed to an angel among the Christmas figures on the windowsill.

“You see,” Mama began, “some angels are the messengers of God. Sometimes they bring a special message to a special person. Gabriel brought the wonderful news to Mary that she would give birth to Jesus.”

"Or," Mama went on, "some angels bring news for everyone. Like when angels appeared to shepherds in the field with the message that Jesus was born in Bethlehem. The shepherds were told they would find Mary and Joseph with Jesus, lying in a manger."

"Those angels were pretty busy!" said Brother.
"And they weren't done yet," said Mama.

"Angels can bring messages that warn of danger too," continued Mama. "When the Wise Men journeyed from afar to worship Jesus and bring him precious gifts, an angel came to Joseph in a dream. He warned him of the evil King Herod, telling him to flee to Egypt with Mary and the child."

"So angels look after us and protect us from danger?" asked Sister.

"That's right," said Papa. "As the Bible says in Psalm 91, 'For he will command his angels concerning you to guard you in all your ways.'"

The cubs were very thoughtful as they went back outside to play. The snow had stopped falling and the sun was peeking out. A long golden shaft of sunlight broke from the clouds and shone down upon their little angel of snow.

“Merry Christmas!” said Sister, turning to Brother and Honey.

“And Merry Christmas to you!” said Brother to Sister and Honey.

“Christmas!” cried Honey. “YAY!”

Brother and Sister gave Honey a big hug and then they all chased each other, laughing and shouting, through the snow.

Here are more stories to read about angels in the Bible!

1. Jacob's Dream—Genesis 28. Angels ascend and descend from heaven.
2. Gideon in Ophrah—Judges 6. An angel appears to Gideon under an oak tree and commands him to save Israel.
3. Elijah in the Wilderness—1 Kings 19. An angel brings food to Elijah.
4. Daniel in the Lions' Den—Daniel 6. God sends an angel to shut the lions' mouths when Daniel is thrown into the lions' den.
5. Peter in Prison—Acts 12. An angel releases Peter from prison.
6. The Angels of the Apocalypse—Revelation. Angels prepare for the coming of the Kingdom.

"It is more blessed to give
than to receive."
Acts 20:35

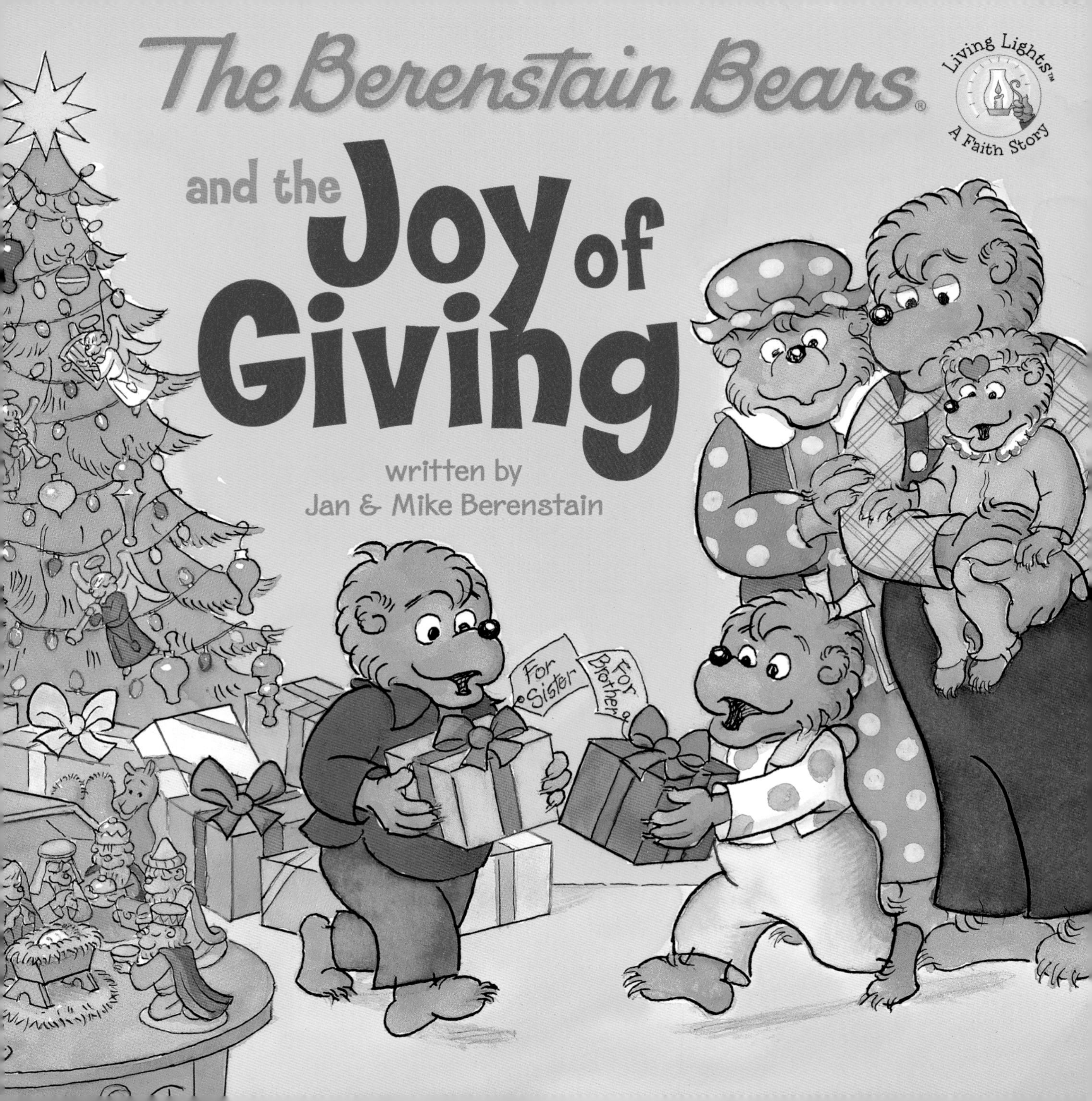
The Berenstain Bears®
and the Joy of Giving
written by
Jan & Mike Berenstain
Living Lights™
A Faith Story
For Sister
For Brother

It was the week before Christmas, and all over Bear Country everyone was busy getting ready for the big day. They were Christmas shopping and Christmas decorating and Christmas *everything*.

Down at the Chapel in the Woods, the cubs of Bear Country were busy getting ready for their Christmas Eve play.

It was *The Story of the First Christmas,* and Brother and Sister had an important role. They were to be the camel of the three wise bears. Sister was the front end of the camel, and Brother brought up the rear. They thought it was the best costume ever.

Missus Ursula, their Sunday school teacher, was directing. “All right, Wise Bears,” she called, “enter, stage right!”

The three wise bears came on stage. They carried gifts and wore long robes, crowns, and fake beards. They followed the Christmas star made of foil-covered cardboard that hung above the stage. The First Wise Bear was played by Sammy Bruno who had a loose front tooth that made him a little hard to understand.

"A thtar! A thtar!" he cried. "I thee a thtar!"

Missus Ursula sighed. "Okay, camel," she called. "You're on!"

Sister and Brother followed the three wise bears. But it was hard to see out of the costume, and Sister accidentally knocked over a palm tree. The three wise bears tripped, going down in a tangle.

“Oh, dear! Oh, dear!” said Missus Ursula. “Will we ever be ready?”

“Sorry, Missus Ursula,” said Sister, poking her head out. “It’s hard to see in there.”

“I’ll need to make your peepholes bigger,” said Missus Ursula. “That’s enough for today, cubs. It’s time to go home.”

The cubs took off their costumes and went into the chilly evening air.

"Brrr!" shivered Sister. "It's beginning to feel a lot like Christmas!"

"Yeah," agreed Brother, "and looking that way, too."

The whole neighborhood was decorated for Christmas. Sister and Brother walked home in the soft glow of many colored lights.

The next day, the Bear family went shopping. It was time for Brother and Sister to pick out a few special gifts. This year they had two crisp ten-dollar bills from Grizzly Gramps and Gran to spend on others.

Of course, Brother and Sister hoped they would have some money left for themselves. Sister was saving for a brand-new Bearbie doll, and Brother wanted a special rubber band-powered model airplane.

Papa and Honey helped Brother do his shopping while Mama went with Sister. Brother picked out a Bearbie doll outfit that he found on sale for Sister, and Sister bought a small airplane model for Brother. Each cost just a few dollars.

Mama and Papa thought that maybe each cub should have spent more money on one another.

"What about the joy of giving?" whispered Mama to Papa. "It seems Brother and Sister only care about the joy of getting."

"True," agreed Papa, "but let's not interfere. They'll learn about the joy of giving for themselves."

Over the next few days, Christmas excitement in Bear Country grew and grew. Brother and Sister could hardly wait. They were going to be a camel and get lots of presents too.

Play rehearsals went well. Sister could see better out of the bigger peepholes, and everyone knew their lines. But it was still a little hard to understand Sammy Bruin.

When Christmas Eve finally arrived, practically everyone in Bear Country jammed the Chapel in the Woods to see the cubs perform. A hush fell as the curtain opened and the play began.

First, the angel Gabriel came to Mary telling her that she would give birth to Jesus.

Then Joseph and Mary journeyed to Bethlehem where the innkeeper gave them shelter in a stable.

There, Mary gave birth to a tiny baby who was laid in a manger.

An angel of the Lord appeared to the shepherds, sharing the good news of Jesus' birth so they could go and worship the newborn King.

Finally, the three wise bears and their faithful camel trooped on stage. The foil-covered Christmas star hung high above the stable, sparkling in the spotlight.

"A star! A star! I see a star!" Sammy said clearly. His lose tooth had come out backstage.

The three wise bears kneeled before Mary, Joseph, and Jesus. The shepherds and the angel joined them.

Everyone bowed low before the tender baby. The three wise bears opened their treasures and gave Jesus their precious gifts.

The audience grew very still. Then someone in the back began to softly sing:

Silent night, Holy night,
All is calm, all is bright...

And the rest of the audience joined in near the end:

Sleep in heavenly peace,
Sleep in heavenly peace.

Peeking out of the camel costume, tears came to Sister's and Brother's eyes. It seemed they had never understood the joy of giving until that moment. All the gifts of all the Christmases of all the years went back to those first gifts given to the tiny baby long ago.

The Christmas Eve play was over, and the audience cheered. Everyone felt the true spirit of Christmas had been with them that night.

On Christmas morning, Brother and Sister led the family downstairs, bright and early. But instead of heading to their own piles of presents, they went to their gifts for each other.

"Merry Christmas!" they said, holding out their presents.

"From one end of the camel to the other," said Brother.

"Thanks!" laughed Sister. "You're a first-rate backup."

Brother and Sister were delighted with their gifts and gave each other big bear hugs. Honey opened her presents, and Brother and Sister joined in. In the back of their minds, though, they were still thinking about the money they had left over from their shopping trip.

Later that morning, the family went to the Chapel in the Woods for the Christmas Day service. A light snow covered the ground, and all of Bear Country glistened in the sun.

On the way, Sister and Brother noticed a group of bears playing Christmas carols. They were collecting money for the needy in a big black pot. Brother and Sister looked at each other, dug into their pockets, and dropped all of their money into the pot.

Mama and Papa smiled with pride.

"You know what the Good Book says," Mama told them. "'It is more blessed to give than to receive.'"

"We know," said Brother. "We receive an awful lot, so it's time we gave some of it back."

“Look!” said Sister, feeling in her pocket. “I still have a quarter.”

Honey reached for it, and Sister put it in her hand.

Then little Honey, holding onto Papa, toddled over to the big black pot and dropped the quarter in. The bears playing music paused.

“Merry Christmas!” they all said.

“Merry Christmas!” answered the Bear family.

Activities and Questions from Brother and Sister Bear

Talk about it:

1. How do you feel when you give a gift to someone? How do you feel when someone gives you a gift?

2. What is the greatest gift that you have ever received? What made it great?

3. Talk about your family's gift-giving traditions and why it is important to give to others?

4. We know that Jesus is God's great gift to the world. Do you think God wants something in return? Did he hold anything back when he gave us his son?

Get out and do it:

1. Design a thank-you card for God. Let him know how much you love and appreciate him and the gift of his son, Jesus.

2. Organize a food drive or coat and blanket drive at your church or school. Choose a group in your community that needs such things and let them know what you are doing. Make posters that let people know who will receive the gift of food or warm clothing. Be sure to include a thank you on the poster.

"Today in the town of David a Savior has been born to you;
he is the Messiah, the Lord. This will be a sign to you:
You will find a baby wrapped in cloths and lying in a manger."

—Luke 2:11-12

The Berenstain Bears®

The Very First Christmas

The Bear cubs love Bible stories and Papa Bear loves reading them to his cubs.

"It's Christmas Eve, cubs. Time to settle down for the night," Papa said.

"Are you going to read to us before we go to sleep, Papa?" asked Sister.

Honey clapped. "Please?" she asked.

Papa smiled. "Of course! How about a story from our storybook Bible?"

"How about the story of the very first Christmas?" asked Brother.

"The very first Christmas it is!"

Storybook
Bible

A young woman named Mary lived in the city of Nazareth. An angel came from God to give Mary wonderful news.

The angel greeted her and said, “You are blessed by the Lord!”

Mary was afraid. But the angel comforted her, saying, “Fear not, for you are special to God. You will have a baby boy who you will name Jesus. He will be called the Son of the Highest.”

Mary said, “How can this be since I am not yet married?”

"With God nothing is impossible," the angel told her.
And Mary said, "I am the servant of the Lord."

At that time, everyone in the Holy Land was to be counted and put on a list. Mary was going to marry Joseph whose family came from Bethlehem. So they had to travel to Bethlehem to be counted, even though it was almost time for Mary to have her baby.

When Mary and Joseph got to Bethlehem, it was very crowded. The only place they could find to stay was the stable at an inn. It was warm and dry and that is where Mary had her baby. She wrapped him in cloths and laid him in the manger where the animals ate.

Nearby, shepherds were watching over their flocks. An angel came to them in a bright light, and they were afraid.

"Don't be afraid," said the angel. "I bring good news for everyone. Today, Christ the Lord is born. You will find the baby lying in a manger."

Suddenly, other angels joined him saying, "Glory to God! Peace on earth!"

The shepherds hurried to Bethlehem. They saw Mary and Joseph, with baby Jesus lying in a manger. Then they told everyone they met what they had seen.

"The King has been born!" they all shouted joyfully.

After Jesus was born, three wise men came from the east to the holy city of Jerusalem.

They asked, "Where is the child who is born a king? We have seen his star and followed it to worship him."

King Herod, who ruled the land, heard about the wise men and their journey. He was worried. Who was this child who people called a king? He told the wise men to find the child and when they did, tell him where he was.

The wise men followed the star that went before them. It led them to the house where Mary, Joseph, and Jesus were staying.

The wise men bowed down and worshipped Jesus. They gave him gold and other precious gifts.

God told them in a dream not to go back to King Herod. So they left and traveled back home another way.

An angel came to Joseph in a dream and told him King Herod was angry with them. He was to take Mary and Jesus to safety in Egypt. So, Joseph, Mary, and Jesus traveled to Egypt and lived there until Herod was dead. Then they went back to the town of Nazareth in the Holy Land. And that is where Jesus grew up.

Activities and Questions from Brother and Sister Bear

Talk about it:

1. Why did the angel visit a girl named Mary? What was his message?

2. When the shepherds found out that a special baby had been born, what did they do?

3. Talk about why Jesus' birth is so important to Christians everywhere.

Get out and do it:

1. As a family, build a diorama showing the first Christmas. Use a large shoebox and any art supplies you have available. Be sure to include the angels and shepherds in your scene.

2. Make Christmas greeting cards for people in a neighborhood nursing home or assisted living facility. Be sure to include messages reminding people how much God loves us and has done for us—especially during this most holy season.